SEDUCING THE FAE KING

A FAE SURROGATES STORY

KAYLA ST. JAMES

FAE Surrogates

KAYLA ST. JAMES

1

———

LIANA

I knew I shouldn't be lurking in dark corners, but it was impossible not to stop. The royal herald was focused on his task, and the nails between his clenched teeth glinted in the early morning light.

The canvas sack slung over his shoulder bulged with rolls of parchment and my fingers itches to snatch one for myself. He struggled with his hammer and dropped the satchel onto the cobblestone street to give him more range of motion. A roll of parchment tumbled out onto the ground and I inched closer.

The crash of the man's hammer against the first nail made me jump.

Three strikes echoed in my ears.

Then three more for the second nail.

A rooster's strident crow made the man pause, but he turned back to his task and didn't see me as I crouched low and snatched the parchment from the ground.

With the previous scroll clutched tight in my fist I ran as

fast as I could down the street and didn't pause when the herald's shout followed me down the narrow street.

I ducked into an alleyway and pressed myself against the uneven stone wall. The roughness of the hastily applied mortar bit into my shoulder but I barely noticed. I held my breath and counted the frantic beat of my heart.

He's not chasing you, silly goose. Not for this.

I'd just given him less work to do.

My smile felt like more of a grimace, teeth grinding together as I forced my fingers to unclasp and release the parchment. I checked over my shoulder to be certain that I was alone, but no one was awake this early… at least no one who cared what I was doing. I unrolled it slowly, flinching at each crackle of the parchment.

A flake of golden paint fluttered down onto the sleeve of my woolen dress and I gnawed on my lip as I stared at the beautifully inked letters.

These announcements were definitely official. I wanted to run my fingertips over the gilded and illuminated letters, but couldn't bring myself to do it. They looked like what I'd always imagined the sacred scrolls kept in the oracle's temple high above the royal citadel looked like.

Too fine for someone like me to look at.

That's what Mistress Beyra always said.

But she said that about everything.

What if this was what I was meant for?

"His illustrious Majesty, Venali Leonan seeks a loyal subject to bear his child."

I said the words slowly, my voice hushed and reverent as I struggled to read the words. I could read well enough, but the words were inked in a fanciful hand and the swirls and flourishes added to the letters made them difficult to read with confidence.

I frowned at the page as I whispered the words.

"Bear his child."

It seemed simple enough. The three kings of Kraterra, powerful royal brothers born of surrogates chosen from the women of the kingdom. The women would be faithful servants of the kingdom. Hopeful beauties. High born fae looking for power and influence.

And me.

To be chosen by the king was a singular honor.

It was a tradition that had been passed down for generations.

Three kings who would take no wives and seek their heirs elsewhere.

I swallowed hard and focused on the words.

"His Majesty will choose his surrogate on the eve of the Feast of the Stars—"

My stomach knotted unexpectedly.

The Feast of the Stars was only a few days away.

My hand tightened on the edge of the parchment and I cursed as I released my grip and tried to smooth out the deep creases I'd made in the fine paper. I rolled it up as tightly as I could and winced as I realized flecks of gold paint had stuck to my fingertips.

I tucked the scroll into a pocket in my woolen skirt and brushed my finger against the rough fabric to brush away the remnants of the paint.

The king would make his choice in a few days' time. I had to work quickly.

"**W**hat do you know about the royal surrogates?

The question was stupid, and I could taste it on my tongue as soon as I said the words.

The woman who peeled potatoes next to me snorted.

"You mean you don't know?"

I shrugged and picked up another potato. "What's to know?"

"You're a fool if you don't," she snapped.

"Maybe I'm a fool."

"I could have guessed that for free."

I glared at the water in the metal pail between my knees. So many potatoes. I didn't even like potatoes. My hands were wrinkled and ugly from the water, and my fingers were numb from the cold. The Feast of the Stars couldn't come at a worse time. Winter festivals were always terrible for servants.

The lady of the house would have a magnificent party and the wealthy and powerful guests would be uncountable. I wouldn't see any of them, of course... I wasn't even permitted to touch the finished delicacies and plates that would be taken up to the banquet hall.

I should have been grateful that I'd been given a paring knife with a handle made from the pearls collected from the inland sea that lapped against Kraterra's western shore. At least that's what I'd been told.

"Please," I whispered.

The woman next to me sighed.

"You're just like every moon-eyed girl in the Citadel's shadow."

"I'm not," I muttered and dropped another potato into the bucket. The water splashed over my knee and I frowned at the stain as the cold, salted well-water soaked into the cloth and sent a shiver up my spine.

The woman chuckled. "What do you want to know?" The glint in her eye was the only encouragement I needed, and I leaned forward.

"Everything," I whispered.

Her eyebrow rose slightly. "Where are you from?" she asked.

"I don't know," I answered honestly. "But I'm here now."

"Mmm... I don't know."

"Please," I begged, all thoughts of shame or pretense were shoved away in my desperation. "I want to know. Why would any woman volunteer for... That?"

The woman eyed me carefully as she peeled a potato with expert precision and tossed it into my bucket. The cold water splashed up and hit my cheek, but I didn't flinch away.

She shook her head. "If I were a younger woman..."

"Would you have gone?" I asked quickly.

"What woman wouldn't?" she scoffed. "I was a beauty in my younger days, I could have turned the eye of a king."

I could see it... Even though she was well into the winter of her life, the woman peeling potatoes next to me in the kitchen yard had bright golden eyes and silver-gray hair that fell in a thick braid over her shoulder. The lines around her eyes were laugh lines, and her smile was quick and bright.

"So why didn't you try?"

She shrugged casually. "It's all about who you know, girl," she scoffed. "It takes more than a pretty face to qualify. They're not just offering a night with a king, it's more than that."

"So... what happens? If they're chosen?"

"A life of luxury, so I'm told," she sighed and dropped the

potato she held into the bucket. Water splashed again and soaked into my dress, but I didn't care. "It's a rare thing to be chosen as a royal surrogate. I dreamed of it for years, but then life stepped in." She pointed her peeling knife at me. "But don't you go getting any ideas. You're not fit for that—"

A flare of indignation rose up inside me. "What's that supposed to mean?"

The woman laughed as I stood up. Water splashed on the ground as I knocked the bucket aside with my boot.

"Don't take it personally, girl. That life's not meant for the likes of us."

"We'll see about that," I snapped.

Stupidly, perhaps, I'd been hoping for an ally, or at least a voice that would confirm what I believed — that I could be chosen.

That I could leave this life behind.

But what the older woman *had* given me was a glimpse of the answer I sought. The royal surrogates were well treated and lived in luxury after their duty to the Jeweled Throne was complete. There was no expectation of a relationship, or service to the king... just a life of blissful excess and ease.

That was what I wanted.

A child was a small price to pay.

2
———————

The apothecary shop was small, but the dirty windows were crowded with a jumble of bottles and scrolls that filled me with a delicious sort of nervousness that twisted low in my belly.

There was no bell over the door, and the hinges creaked loudly as I entered. The roughness of the wood but into my fingers as I pushed hard against the door to open it wider.

The crackle of parchment and the clatter of falling bottles made me flinch. The room was piled high with crumpled pieces of parchment, bundles of crumbling herbs, and mysterious bags and pouches all covered with a thick layer of dust.

I coughed and blinked hard to keep the swirl of it out of my eyes.

"Hello?"

I whispered it, almost hoping that the shop was empty. Nervousness could give way to fear in an instant.

I swallowed hard and stepped into the shop. The door swing closed behind me as soon as I released my grip and I scrambled out of the way as it slammed closed and a small avalanche of parchment and bottles cascaded to the floor.

"What are you doing?

The voice was commanding, but as brittle as the parchment that littered the floor.

Cheeks burning, I scrambled to push some of the mess back into the pile behind the door, but it slipped didn't around me and only made matters worse.

How was I going to get out?

"I— I'm sorry," I stammered as I pushed at the parchment tower again. "I thought you'd be able to help me."

"With what," the voice snapped.

I gave the parchment one final push and winced as another bottle tumbled down and rattled across the uneven floorboards. With a grimace, I pulled the royal notice out of my pocket and held it out as I strode toward what I hoped was the shop's main counter.

"I have this," I exclaimed. "I want to be chosen as a surrogate."

Dusty laughter echoed in my ears and I glared at the parchment covered counter. "Tell me why I can't," I demanded.

A slender hand emerged, fingertips stained black with ink, and pushed a stack of scrolls off the counter. I don't know why I'd expected someone... different to own a shop like this, but I shouldn't have been surprised.

The shop had a distinct flair that I should have recognized immediately. Collections of bottles and scrolls, piles of glittering objects, mysterious casks and boxes, bound in iron to keep fairies out, all of it covered in cobwebs and a thick layer of dust.

A goblin with silverblue rings fastened to its long dark

hair stared back at me with large, defiant eyes that shone silver in the dim light.

It was impossible to know how old goblins were unless they told you, and their secrets cost more copper coins than I would ever possess.

Ink-stained nails tapped on the stained wooden counter as the goblin stared at me, calculating.

"Well?" I choked out.

"You look young enough," the goblin said. "Are you fertile?"

"I— How should I know?"

His mouth curved. "Have y'had a babe?"

I made a face. "No."

"A serving wench, then." It wasn't a question.

"I work for Lady—"

The goblin held up a broad hand. "It doesn't matter."

"Can you help me?"

The goblin leaned on the counter and beckoned me forward. I complied with halting steps and flinched as the creature snatched the royal announcement from my fingers. He read it carefully, glancing up at me every so often, and I fidgeted as I waited.

"Well?"

He rolled the parchment carefully and handed it back to me. "Why should I?"

I hadn't thought of that. I only had a few coppers in my pocket. Not enough to buy anyone's silence, or help.

"Can you just... What if I just bought some herbs and you pretend you didn't see me?"

The goblin's dark brow rose. "It takes quite a lot for me to forget a face. Especially a beautiful one."

"I just—" I shoved the parchment into my bodice and

fumbled in my pocket for the coins that I'd brought. They clattered on the rough wood as I threw them down. "What can you give me?"

His tongue clicked as he looked at the coins and then back at me. "Advice."

I grabbed for the coins, but he swept them out of sight before I could snatch them away.

"It's not enough to *want* to be a surrogate," he said. "What was your plan? Overdose yourself on some tea to open your womb and then, what, throw yourself at the Fae King when his carriage passes by and hope to catch his eye before you're trampled under the hooves of the royal horses?

I glared back at the goblin.

"No."

"So you didn't have a plan?"

No.

"I—"

The goblin chuckled and shook his head. "You have to be chosen," he said. "The Lords of the Jeweled Throne choose their surrogates carefully. To even be considered is a great honor. Surely even someone like you would know that."

"I do," I whispered.

Furious tears pricked my lashes, and I blinked them away. I *was* angry now. Mostly with myself. How could I have even hoped that I would be chosen?

A kitchen wench as a royal surrogate.

How ridiculous.

No wonder the only other woman I'd told about my ambitions had laughed at me.

"Do you even know where the surrogates are chosen from? And how much the wealthy families pay to have their daughters put forward for the king's scrutiny?"

I shook my head and stared at the dusty floor. An emerald green beetle crawled across a scrap of parchment and disappeared into a crack between two floorboards.

A desperate wish that the building was full of wood-boring beetles and that it would crash down on my head at that very moment flitted through my mind and the goblin chuckled.

"It's a brothel, you know."

"A what?"

The goblin's silver shadowed eyes glinted in the weak light. "The place where the king chooses his surrogates."

"Oh."

"You thought they would be taken to the citadel?"

"I— I don't know."

"Of course. Why would you?" The goblin sighed. "The announcements never reveal the sordid details." He held up three long fingers. "The king will choose three young women."

"Three," I blurted out. "But—"

"The king isn't looking for love, little one," the goblin said. A silverblue glint was revealed in his quick smile. "The vessel is not important. Only the child."

"That's why I wanted the herbs," I said slowly.

Why hadn't he told me to leave?

"Ah, but what does it matter how ripe your womb is if you can't catch the king's eye?" the goblin asked.

His ink-stained fingernails tapped on the rough wooden counter.

Suddenly, it dawned on me.

The right question.

"But— could you get me into the brothel?"

The goblin's eyes glinted. "Perhaps."

"Whatever price—"

"You have nothing I want, girl," he snorted. But my heart lurched in my chest as he looked me up and down once more and leaned his elbows on the counter. "However..."

"However?"

"I might know someone who would be interested in your... ambition."

I swallowed the lump in my throat and nodded. "What do I have to do?"

⬥

The apothecary had given me what I'd asked for in the end; a packet of herbs to make into a foul-tasting tea that I was to drink twice a day. I regretted every sip, and hated the way it burned in my stomach, but if it would get me what I wanted?

Well, then I could bear anything.

Every morning before the sun came up, and each night when all the lights in the house were out, I read and re-read the royal proclamation. And twice a day I grimaced as I drank my tea. When all the herbs were gone, it was time to meet the goblin's associate.

Dawn was pale and gray, and cold. Winter was on the edge of the wind, and I had no intention of spending the most brutal months of the year working my fingers to the bone.

Not this year. Not next year.

Never again.

"Midnight at the Monarch," I whispered as I tossed the empty paper packet onto the coals that glowed in the remnants of my fire and gulped down the dregs of the last cup of tea.

It was difficult enough to perform my duties with any sense of urgency on a regular day. But now that my mind was fixed on the day I would meet whichever shadowy figure would change my life... it was so much harder to concentrate.

I did my best to keep out of sight, and keep out of everyone's way as much as I could. It didn't mean I escaped every abuse hurled my way, but I escaped the ones that could have meant I would miss my appointment.

The Monarch.

A brothel, of course, but one of the best establishments in the city. I'd seen the women who worked there—gloriously ethereal creatures with glowing skin, rippling cascades of thick hair, straight white teeth... graceful beauties from all corners of the kingdom.

A fortunate few.

And I wanted to be one of them.

More than anything.

Midnight.

I crept through the streets and hoped that I hadn't been followed. If I was discovered now, everything would be ruined. This meeting was my chance to get my foot in the proverbial door, and I was willing to do anything to get through.

The goblin had said something about being examined... but I didn't know what that meant. Would I be poked and prodded with medical precision, or was it something more... sinister?

The Monarch was well lit, and that made me even more

nervous. Torches burned in niches in the stone wall that surrounded the building and expensive candles made from the perfumed wax of the silverbees that hummed in the wildflower fields beyond the city walls burned in every window.

I had only smelled those candles once in my life and I vowed to have them burning every hour of the day when I was made a royal surrogate.

I had spent every single gold coin already in my mind.

There was no sense in being frugal. I would have more money than I would ever know how to spend. Why not be extravagant?

I smiled as the thought of being in a room filled with soft candlelight that smelled like a summer field filled my mind. Anything was preferable to shivering under a thin blanket in a hut that let more snow in through the chinks in the wood than it kept out.

The street wasn't empty, but I couldn't wait any longer.

Drunken melodies and laughter floated on the chill autumn air, and I rushed across the street toward the elegant building. The carefully carved and painted wooden sign swung on golden chains over the wide doorway.

I hesitated for only a moment before I knocked on the door with a firm hand. There was no time to be shy.

The door opened almost instantly, and I jumped back as a broad figure filled the space. Dark eyes glared down at me, and then the man's expression softened, but only a little.

"Servants go around the back, girl," he growled.

My shoulders straightened. This was my last chance to run away. But I hadn't drunk that foul tasting tea for nothing. "I'm not a servant," I choked out. "I'm here to see Artin."

The man smirked as he looked me up and down, and then the door closed in my face with a resounding *thud*.

"Hey!"

I smashed my fist against the door.

The door opened again and a different man, older than the first, and with a leaner bulk. He still towered over me.

"I was sent by Tannyl," I blurted out. "You have to let me in. I'm here to see Artin!"

"Are you just," he said. His smile was sly as his gaze slid over me. "And why should I let you in?"

I glared up at him. "I was told to come here at midnight— I'm here. Let me in."

I glanced over my shoulder, suddenly nervous that I might be seen loitering in the doorway of a brothel when I should see to my Lady's instructions for the kitchen staff for the morning...

"Please," I hissed. "Let me in."

The man's mouth twisted in a shadow of a smile before he opened the door wide enough to allow me to dash inside. I had to brush against him as I did so, and his chuckle made my cheeks burn.

I was grateful to be inside and away from prying eyes, but I wasn't sure what I was supposed to do now.

"Tannyl sent me," I stammered, and pulled the piece of parchment the goblin had given me from a pocket in my cloak. I held it with a shaking hand and the man snatched it out of my grasp and read it quickly.

"Sent you to what?" he asked.

I blinked at him in surprise. "To— I'm supposed to ask for Artin. That's all I know."

"You're at a brothel at midnight," he said as he stepped closer. He was roguishly handsome in the soft light from the lanterns. With dark hair that swept over his forehead and a scar that marred his left eyebrow and disappeared in the hair that covered his elegantly pointed ears.

"What usually happens to beautiful girls in brothels?" he murmured. A long-fingered hand stroked along my cheek, and his thumb brushed over my lower lip.

I knew what happened at brothels.

Was this the examination?

It couldn't be.

I pushed his hand away and ignored the heat that flared in my stomach at the gentleness of his touch. I'd only ever known roughness, but I wasn't here for this...

"I'm here to see Artin," I repeated firmly. "I want to be a royal surrogate, and you don't look like any king I've ever seen."

Anger flashed in his dark eyes, but only for a moment. "A surrogate," he said. "You don't look like the kind of girl who usually has such ambitions."

I lifted my chin. "And?"

His chuckle made my throat tighten.

"And nothing," he said. "Follow me."

3

———

$\mathcal{H}$e shoved the parchment back into my hands and strode down a stone corridor. I hurried to keep up with him and wondered if I'd insulted him — did it matter? Had I passed a test?

"Wait for me," I hissed.

"Keep up," he called back.

A wooden door opened, and I stumbled on the uneven stones. He stepped into a room lit with elegant lamps, and the smell of the silverbeeswax filled my nostrils and made me feel a little dizzy.

Intoxicating.

That would be my life. When I was a royal surrogate, that exotic scent would follow me everywhere.

The young man's handsome face peered back at me. "Hurry up, girl. Don't keep Artin waiting."

I swallowed hard, wiped my palms on my bodice, and walked toward the room with as much boldness as I could manage. They didn't have to know I was afraid.

Was I afraid?

Of course I was.

No one knew where I was… if something happened—

Stop it.

Walk.

I didn't look at him as I entered the room, but he chuckled when I flinched as the door slammed shut behind me.

A woman with long dark blue hair sat at an elegantly carved wooden table piled neatly with stacks of scrolls, parchment, green glass inkwells, and long quills made from fanciful feathers of birds I'd never seen before.

My mistress' most expensive quills were made from ruffed pheasant feathers and I only knew that because of the hushed tones that the other girls spoke in when they described the finery, they were permitted to dust when they entered her bedchamber.

"Artin?" I said. "I was sent to see you—"

"I know," the woman said, but she didn't look up from the letter she was writing. "Royal surrogates. I didn't realize how quickly the months were passing until the proclamations were sent out."

She set down her quill with a heavy sigh and dusted the parchment with fine sand before handing it to a servant who stood nearby.

The young man who had brought me to her lounged against one wall. I didn't like the way he watched me. His eyes were hungry.

A weirwolf looking for a meal.

"What's your name, girl?"

"Liana," I replied.

The woman made a face. "I see. You have Tannyl's recommendation?"

I pulled the parchment out of my pocket and held it out.

Artin crossed her arms over her chest and stared at me. Feeling like a fool, I stumbled forward and dropped it on the table in front of her.

She picked it up with two fingers and frowned delicately at the goblin's deceptively beautiful script.

"And what did he tell you?"

"About what?"

"About— Nothing? Did he tell you nothing?"

I swallowed hard. The scent of the candles was making me feel dizzy. But I couldn't remember if I'd eaten anything that day...

"He gave me some tea," I choked out. "I want to be a surrogate."

"Yes, I gathered that," Artin said with a small smile that faded away so quickly it was as though I had imagined its presence. "And you drank it all?"

"Down to the last leaf," I replied quickly.

"Good. Then you will be ripe," she said.

She rose from her seat and crossed the room to drop the piece of parchment into the small fire that crackled in the hearth.

"Ripe—" I whispered.

"Yes, of course," Artin said smoothly. "What good are you to the Kings of the Jeweled Throne if you cannot bear a child? They need you to be fertile. You will have a month to prove your worth. And you will not be the only one vying for the king's attentions."

"I—"

Artin moved closer and trailed a hand over my shoulder. She unpinned my cloak, and I forced myself to stand still as it dropped to the floor. Artin dragged her hand through my hair and frowned at the tangles before she gripped my chin and gazed into my eyes.

It would have been easy to look away, but I couldn't. Her eyes were clear and a hypnotic shade of gray that I had never seen before.

"Good skin," she mused. "The hair could use some work, and she smells like a stable lad."

The servants covered their laughter with their hands, and the man who had brought me into the building chuckled in agreement.

Artin's scrutiny traveled down my body, and I flinched as she rubbed her fingers over my collarbone.

"Hold her," she said briskly.

The angular, dark-eyed man did as commanded, and I wondered if he did it with any enjoyment. His fingers closed over my arms and held me in place as Artin pulled up my skirts. I sucked in a breath as her warm palms rubbed over my thighs and brushed dangerously close to the juncture of my thighs.

"What—"

"Be still," she hissed.

"What do you think?" the young man asked. His mouth was close to my ear, and the depth of his voice made me shiver.

Artin frowned as she straightened and rubbed a careless hand over my breasts before she tugged at the laces of my bodice to expose my bare flesh to the room. My cheeks burned, and I struggled in the man's grip.

Warm hands rubbed over my breasts and pinched at my nipples, which hardened to dark pink peaks. I bit my lip to keep from swearing at her, and Artin's pale eyes flickered to mine.

"The tea has done its work," she said. "She may as well be in heat."

"Delicious," the young man murmured.

I squirmed out of his grasp and grabbed for my bodice to re-tie it.

"She's fiery," Artin said as she walked back to her table and took her seat once more. "The king will be pleased to have a bit of a challenge. Has he ever taken a servant before?"

"Not in a place like this," the young man said. I could feel the smile in his voice, but I refused to look at him. He didn't deserve my anger.

"She'll need to be bathed," Artin said. She pulled a scroll from one of the piles at her elbow and picked up a quill that matched the color of her hair. The nib scratched across the parchment. "Take her upstairs."

"As you say," the young man replied.

"Not you, Jaren," she snapped. "She's not for you to play with. She's royal property now. Unless the king decides he doesn't want her."

"What happens then?" I choked out, scarcely able to believe that my plan had worked.

Artin looked up briefly. "If the king doesn't choose you, you'll be tossed out into the street where you belong."

My jaw clenched. I don't know what I'd expected her to say, but it wasn't that.

My mistress would never allow me back to the house, especially because I'd disappeared without a word. There was no one I could send a message to—no one would care. They would say I'd run away.

I grabbed my cloak from the stone floor and held it tightly to my chest as one of the servants came forward and took hold of my elbow.

"Come with me, girl, we'll wash the stables off you," the woman said brightly.

All I could do was stumble along beside her.

Jaren opened the door, and I made the mistake of glancing at him as I passed. His wink chilled me to the bone, and I didn't like the sharpness of his smile.

I would have to watch out for him. There was no telling what he might do... and the confirmation of my 'ripeness' only seemed to make him more interested in what I had to offer.

Despite the danger he presented, he was handsome enough that on any other day, I might have considered it.

But I wasn't here for any diversion... I had a purpose. But as Artin had made very clear, my new status was a precarious one, and if I wanted to keep my new position, I was going to have to be on my guard.

⸙

Two days.

Two days of pampering, scrubbing, oiling, scraping, massaging, and curling had changed the person I saw when I looked in the silvered mirror that sat on the vanity table in front of me. The room was sparsely decorated, but it was finer than anything I'd ever been in. The bed was heavenly, and the women who had brought me there said that I'd slept for longer than anyone else who had come to the Monarch.

I stared at my reflection and touched the jeweled chain that had been draped across my forehead and wound through my hair to hold it back from my face.

"His Majesty is coming today." The bright voice of the

woman who had brought my breakfast announced from the doorway. "Artin will want you looking your best, and I'm to remind you to be on your best behavior."

"Best behavior?"

I didn't know how to act in front of a king. "Are you going to teach me how to curtsey?" I asked as she set down a cup and a pewter jug. The cider she poured smelled sweet and crisp, and I grabbed for the cup eagerly.

The woman frowned, and I felt a twinge of guilt for never asking her name. She'd seen me naked on more than one occasion and had spent a good deal of time in my company... Maybe my manners did need work.

"Artin will explain all the rules, but I'll give you a piece of advice," she leaned closer, "be unexpected."

I looked at her in surprise. "How— How would I do that?"

She shrugged and turned away to gather up my sleeping robe and tucked it into a basket of other linens that needed washing. She pointed to the bed and the velvet gown that had been laid out for me. "Get dressed. You won't need my help. And don't touch your hair!"

I pulled my nervous fingers away from the jewels on my head and nodded obediently.

"Hurry! Artin will call for you sooner than you think!"

She swept out of the room with her arms full, and I jumped up out of my chair and hurried to the bed. The dark blue velvet gown was more beautiful than anything I'd ever worn, and I rubbed my fingers over the smooth fabric and the intricately embroidered pattern of interlocking leaves and vines.

Three vines and three star-shaped flowers picked out in silver thread. The symbols of the royal court. Three kings, forever bound by blood.

I would be one of the ones chosen to bear the next generation of royalty.

I would bear the king an heir.

A servant girl from the gutters in the bed of a king. It was almost too impossible to believe.

"You're not in his bed yet," I muttered as I shrugged out of the silken robe that I'd been given and picked up the gown. It was heavy. Yards of rich fabric that would have purchased food for a month... and I would wear it once.

I stepped into the gown and sucked in a breath as I realized how closely it fit and how much of my skin was exposed. My arms were covered, but the bodice dipped so low that the blush of my nipples was almost visible above the intricate embroidery work.

The bodice hugged my ribs intimately, and as I laced it up with shaking fingers, I knew I shouldn't have been surprised. I wasn't here to be a royal lady. I was a concubine. A surrogate. A means to an end.

The king would choose from the most delectable specimens that Artin had collected at his command, and I had to be one of them. If being chosen meant parading naked in front of him, I would do it. For now, I was grateful to be encased in shimmering blue velvet with assets that were sure to catch his eye.

I turned to look in the mirror and almost gasped at my reflection. No one at my former mistress' house would recognize me. I barely recognized myself.

Good.

I wasn't that version of Liana anymore, and I had no intention of going back.

4

―――――

rtin paced in front of us, a collection of beautiful young women that she had summoned to the Monarch's reception room. The walls were hung with expensive tapestries, and the red-gold light of sunset streamed through the stained glass windows and painted the carpeted floor at our feet in strange patterns.

"When his majesty arrives, you will bow your heads. Do not look at him until he speaks to you. He will speak to each of you in turn, and I will tolerate no attempts to draw his attention away from the others... This choice is the king's to make. You are not here to flirt; you are here for one purpose only."

I swallowed the lump in my throat and remembered what the serving woman had said to me.

Be unexpected.

The other young women had long family histories, rich and powerful bloodlines... What did I have?

Artin could have turned me away. The goblin could have

refused to give me the herbs I'd demanded of him. That meant something.

It had to.

"When the king makes his decision, those chosen will stay here at the Monarch for thirty days, or until there is a confirmed pregnancy. You will be my guests, but you will become the property of the Jeweled Throne. Do I make myself clear?"

The others nodded, and I did the same. My palms were cold, and I pressed them against my skirts to keep from fidgeting. Nervousness crept up my spine as iron-shod hooves clattered over the cobblestones outside.

"It is time," Artin snapped. "Remember, you will not look at his Majesty until he speaks to you. Answer his questions, but say no more."

Murmured agreement followed her announcement, but I stayed silent.

Artin gestured to the men behind her, men who looked more like guards than anything, and they opened the door to allow her to step into the corridor.

"Does anyone know which king will be coming?" someone asked.

"King Venali," someone replied. "Didn't you read the proclamation?"

"But which one is he?"

"Hush, does it matter?"

"They're all terribly handsome, aren't they? I would take any of them."

"Hush!"

Footsteps in the corridor, muffled voices, and Artin's musical laughter echoed beyond the door. My heart pounded in my chest and I tried to keep still. Shoulders back, chin high. I might not belong here, but I wasn't going to leave empty-handed.

"Majesty, this way, if you please," Artin said from just outside the doorway. "There are seven potentials awaiting your decision."

"Seven." The king's voice rumbled, and a shiver crept down my arms. "I trust you have chosen according to my requests?"

"As ever, Majesty," Artin replied smoothly.

The guards entered the room first and checked all corners and behind the tapestries for any hint of danger. Artin's expression was unreadable as she walked at the king's side, and I clutched at my skirts as the king appeared. He was almost too tall for the doorway, and one of the young women barely bit back a gasp as his amber eyes swept over the room.

"I don't know why I doubt you, Artin," he murmured. "It would be impossible to find such a beautiful collection anywhere else in the kingdoms."

"You are too kind, Majesty," Artin replied, but her tone almost made me smile. Artin knew what she was doing. "Please, take your time."

The other young women bowed their heads, but I didn't. The king's eyes swept over us and then lingered on me. His dark hair was pulled back from his forehead and a thick braid secured with a wide gold band fell over his shoulder.

I didn't know what I'd expected a king to look like. Maybe I'd expected a fur-trimmed cloak and a tall crown like the kings in fairy tales and songs... This man looked more like a warrior. He carried himself like one, too.

A scar that split the outer edge of his upper lip marred the smooth skin of his face and tugged his mouth into a half-smile that was sensual and dangerous at the same time. A scar like that could only have come from a terrible wound, and I was fascinated by it.

Leather armor hugged his torso and forearms, and his hand rested on the hilt of the sword at his hip.

"Eyes down," Artin snapped. The other women complied immediately, but I was slower to react. The king moved along the line, pausing to speak softly to each of the young women. I watched him out of the corner of my eye.

He didn't touch all of them — he stopped long enough to rub his fingers along one woman's collarbone before moving away.

I overheard some of their conversation. A question about their families and where they came from. One woman laughed, but stopped herself at a sharp glance from Artin.

When he finally reached me, I looked up into his dark eyes before he had a chance to touch me or speak to me.

"A beauty," he murmured. "What is your name?"

"Liana," I replied quickly. I knew I should have looked away, but I couldn't. "Before you ask, I don't come from a good family, and my father doesn't breed horses."

His lips curved into a smile, and my stomach tightened. "What does he do?"

I shrugged. "I have no idea. I never met him. And my mother died giving birth to me."

The king glanced at Artin, and her lips pressed into a thin line.

"Where did you find this one?" he chuckled.

"She didn't find me," I answered for her, and the king looked at me in surprise.

"Indeed," he said. His eyes were brown, dark, and rich, and I couldn't look away even though I knew I should have.

My cheeks were warm and my heart thundered in my chest.

"Is she fertile?" he asked Artin as though I wasn't even there.

"She is," the brothel owner replied through clenched teeth. "A child would come as sure as spring if you were to take her."

His hand came up to my jaw, and he stroked his fingers along it briefly before his gaze dropped to my breasts. His hand trailed down over my throat, pausing to caress the pulse that thundered there, and then down over the tops of my breasts, pushed even higher by the lacing of the gown.

His palm pressed against my breasts, and even through the fabric of the gown I could feel the heat of his hand. Desire flamed in my belly in an instant, and I had to bite my lip to keep from moaning aloud.

"Promising," he murmured. "Have her made ready."

Artin nodded. "Of course, Majesty." She glanced at me and then at the other girls. "Any of the others?"

His hand was still on my breast, and I leaned forward slightly. "No," he said. "Just her."

"But, Majesty... would you not wish to have more opportunity—"

His hand slipped from my breast as he turned to Artin. "I have made my command."

She averted her eyes and curtseyed as he passed by her. "Of course." When she rose, Artin fixed me with a furious glare before gesturing to the servants, who waited for her instruction.

"Take her to the royal suite," she hissed. "And be quick about it."

My breath caught. Was it really so easy?

A servant took hold of my arm and pulled me away from the other young women. One of the tapestries was pulled back to reveal a hidden door, and I stumbled after the woman who held my arm.

Behind me, the room erupted and filled with outraged voices.

"Her? But I thought he would choose more of us—"

"My lady, shouldn't there be more time—"

The door slammed shut behind us and I tripped on the stone steps as I tried to keep up with the servant's quick pace.

"What— what happens now?" I choked out.

I was overwhelmed with the possibility of what lay before me. I had achieved what I had set out to do—at least part of it.

But the servant didn't answer my question. She just kept climbing.

The stairs seemed to go on forever, and I pressed my hand against the smooth stone wall to keep from falling backward. My legs were weak and my heart pounded in my chest.

I'd done it.

I'd passed the test, and the king had chosen me.

Ahead of me, the servant paused, and the scrape of a key in a lock echoed around me. Another secret door opened, and I hurried to catch up.

The woman huffed impatiently as I squeezed past her and stepped into the room.

"Are there more of these rooms?" I murmured. It was sumptuously decorated, with rich tapestries and an enormous bed covered in thick quilted blankets and embroidered pillows. A table beneath the stained glass window held a pewter jug, two matching goblets, a large bowl of exotic fruit, and a tray of sweet pastries.

"What— What do I do?"

The woman shrugged and unlaced my gown. The door creaked open, and Artin swept into the room. "What else should you do?" she asked. Her voice was sharp, and I flinched as the servant tugged at the gown to drag it down my torso. I crossed my arms over my breasts, and my face warmed with embarrassment.

"The king is coming to breed you," Artin continued. "There is no need for modesty any longer. You will be examined regularly to determine the success of this venture."

The gown slipped down my legs and pooled on the floor around my feet. Without pause, the servant tugged at the ribbon that held my underskirt in place, and it, too, tumbled to the floor, leaving me naked in front of Artin.

The servant pushed me forward, and I stepped out of the gown so she could gather it up in her arms. Artin pulled a small velvet pouch from her belt and drew out a silverblue chain set with long sapphires. She stepped toward me and fastened it around my waist.

I shivered as the cold metal settled against my skin and Artin's fingertips stroked against my naked flesh.

"This is a contract, Liana," she murmured. "And I will expect payment for this favor. I could have turned you out into the street and no one would have said a word. I trust that Tannyl would not have wasted his time, or his precious herbs, on a worthless investment."

"Investment?"

Artin straightened and looked me in the eye. "We will speak about this more in due course... I have a feeling that it will not be long before the king has what he desires. Then we shall talk about your future."

I swallowed hard, but nodded my agreement. I owed the

goblin everything. If he'd turned me away, I would be scraping pots in the freezing dark of the kitchens beneath my mistress' house.

"The king will be here shortly. Make yourself ready. If he is pleased with you, then our next conversation will be an enjoyable one. If not..."

Her voice trailed away, and I had to assume that if the king was displeased, that I would be disposed of and another of the young women who had been passed over would take my place. I couldn't let that happen.

"I understand," I whispered.

"Good."

Artin's smile was bitter as she gripped my wrists and pulled my hands away from my breasts.

"Take some wine, but not too much," she said as she released me and turned away. The servant departed the room first, and I shivered as Artin pulled the door closed behind her.

Wine would calm my nerves.

A fire crackled in the hearth, and the silverbeeswax candles I coveted so much burned in pewter candelabras placed around the room. It smelled heavenly, and I took a shaking breath before I poured two cups of wine with an unsteady hand.

I had come to the Monarch full of bravery, but now that I was here and the king was approaching, all of that bravery melted away.

I stood in front of the fire and barely felt the heat sweep over my bare skin. The sapphires in the chain around my waist glittered in the firelight, and I rubbed my fingers over them gently. The chain was loose now, resting on my hips, but when the king's child was in my belly...

Everything would change.

I held the goblet to my lips and inhaled the scent of the rich, honeyed wine. One small sip was all I allowed myself. I was too nervous to give myself over to the warmth of the liquid. I wanted to be alert for what lay ahead.

The candles beside the bed bathed the room in a soft glow, and I set the goblet of wine on a small table before I climbed up onto the rich coverlet and lay back against the wall of pillows.

The heat that had twisted in my belly when the king touched me flared to life once more. I was waiting for him to come to me. To take me. The ache of knowing what was coming filled me, and my fingers itched to touch my body.

"She's almost in heat."

Artin's words repeated in my mind. That would explain my insatiable cravings for sensuous touch, and the almost constant dampness between my thighs. I was ready to be bred, and I was eager for it.

My hand slid down my body, teasing at my aching nipples, and my eyes drifted closed as I slipped my other hand between my thighs. I imagined how the king would take me. Would he be rough like the warrior I assumed him to be? Or would he be gentle, like a scholar?

My breath came faster and faster as I swirled my fingers over my slick heat as I imagined what the smooth hardness of the king's cock would feel like when it had plunged into my aching pussy.

My breath caught as my fingers moved, and I did not hear the door as it opened.

"I hope I have not disturbed you."

I gasped and sat up, my cheeks burning as the king stepped into the room and closed the door behind him. I had half-expected him to come with a bevy of guards and attendants, and I reached desperately for a pillow to cover my nakedness before I remembered that this was what he wanted.

The smile on his angular face was sly, and the key turned in the lock.

"No, I was only just waiting for you... Majesty."

"So I see."

The king deposited the silver key on the table beside the wine she had poured for him.

"I want you to continue."

I bit my lip as my pussy throbbed. He stared at me with hungry eyes. A wierwolf circling his prey. And I wanted to be devoured.

The king licked his lips and picked up the goblet of wine. As he drank, I spread my legs so that he could see what I was doing.

"That's it," he hissed. "I want you to tell me what you are thinking about while you do it."

I dragged my hands down my body, pausing to pinch and pluck at my nipples, and I didn't stop myself as I moaned at the sensation that rushed through my body. My fingers inched closer to the hot wetness between my legs, and I sighed as my fingers spread my silken folds and teased against my aching clit.

"I was imagining how you would fuck me, Majesty," I said. "How it would feel to have your cock inside me? What your cum would taste like—"

"I won't be wasting a single drop," he said smoothly. "I'm here to sire a child— or have you forgotten?"

I swallowed hard, but didn't stop the movement of my

hand. My fingers dipped into my pussy, stretching and teasing the tender flesh. Gods, I was so ready for him.

"Of course not," I breathed. "But, Majesty, wouldn't you like me to taste you—"

I sucked in a sharp breath as my fingers worked furiously to mimic the motions I hoped he would make and my moan was frustrated as I bit down on my lip.

Was this all he wanted? Surely not.

He wasn't wearing his leather armor anymore, and I wondered what his bare flesh looked like. Would his chest be scarred like his face? Would I ever know what had happened to him?

The king set down his goblet and strode to the bed. I tried to slow the motion of my hand, but it was intoxicating now, and I didn't know if I could stop before my orgasm swept over me. The king's hand flashed out and took hold of my hair, and I sucked in a sharp breath as he held it tightly in his fist, pulling my face toward his groin.

I could see the outline of his cock through his breeches, and I licked my lips in anticipation. He liked what he was watching, that was clear enough.

"Majesty, please—"

I could feel my release climbing, and a moan escaped my lips. The king's hand tightened on my hair and a flash of pleasure and pain rippled through my limbs as my back arched and my hips moved in time with the furious motion of my fingers. Before I realized what had happened, the king had undone his breeches with his free hand and released his rock hard cock.

I opened my mouth eagerly, hungry to taste him.

"Do not stop. I want to watch you fuck yourself while you choke on my cock." Obediently, my fingers resumed their circular motion, dipping in and out of my soaking pussy as the head of the king's cock nudged between my lips and entered my mouth.

His groan of pleasure encouraged me to stay still, and his hand on my hair, pulling me toward him, caused me to take more and more of his smooth length into my mouth.

He was hardness and softness and fiery passion, and my mouth slipped around his manhood until the head of his cock pressed against the back of my throat. He choked me with it briefly before he pulled back, only to test my resolve again.

I moaned deep in my throat, eager to be used, and the king's answering groan told me I was doing exactly what he wanted.

The lazy circles being made by my fingers drove my pleasure higher and higher, and my heart thundered in my chest. The king's cock stiffened in my mouth, and I looked up to see the king frozen, with his head thrown back in ecstasy, before he pulled his cock from my mouth.

My face was wet with tears and saliva, and my pussy throbbed with the need to be filled.

The king released his hold on my hair. "I want you on your hands and knees, girl."

I swallowed hard, gasping for breath, and did as I was told. I bit down hard on my lip as I bent forward and exposed myself to him, presenting the swollen lips of my pussy to him. I fought the urge to flinch as he stroked his hand over my burning skin.

He ran his fingers over my wet, throbbing cleft, teasing me with his tender touch before pushing a finger inside, making me gasp in surprise. My gasp was rewarded with a stinging slap on my ass cheek.

I bit my lip to keep from crying out as he followed the slap with two more in the same place.

He rubbed his hand over the top of my ass and up my back, bending my waist and pressing me down into the softness of the bed.

"Give me your hands."

I hesitated for only a moment before I complied. He pulled my wrists together behind my back and gasped into the coverlet as the king tied them together with a length of velvet. The sensation of the knot tightening against my skin sent a shockwave through my body. My pussy throbbed in response and I pushed my ass back toward him to show him how eager I was to be bred however he wanted me.

The swiftness of the slap that stung my ass next made me cry out in shock, which earned me three more sharp slaps.

I shuddered and moaned, hoping that he would continue his punishment and give me the release I craved. I vibrated with need for him, and pushed my ass toward him again, begging him without words to sink his fingers, or his cock, inside me.

Begging for him to stretch me and make me feel whole before tearing me apart.

As if he had known what I wanted, the king teased my tender opening with his fingers, first one, and then two, sinking them deep into my pussy, plunging them into me with a speed and force that made me cry out.

Every cry was met with a stinging slap, and soon my ass and thighs were burning and I was shuddering with ecstasy. He gripped my ass hard, intensifying the pain and the pleasure at the same time, and I pressed her face into the bed to keep from crying out.

All at once, his hand was soft on my heated skin.

"A determined breeder," he murmured.

"Yes, Majesty," I gasped. He chuckled in response, and I wondered if he was surprised at my eagerness to please him.

He gripped the ribbon that tied my hands together and pulled on them, tugging my chest off the bed and stretching my back, tilting my ass higher, and opening my pussy to him.

"Artin says that you are fertile, and that there will be a child—"

"Yes, Majesty," I moaned. "Take me... let me give you the child you crave."

I moaned softly as I felt the head of his cock press against my shivering opening. I wanted him so badly, needed him inside me. The prolonged wait had driven me almost to the point of madness, and my body hovered on the brink of release.

I struggled to push herself back toward him, to force him to take me, and without warning he plunged deep inside and I cried out as he filled me with his cock again, and again.

Long deep strokes brought me to the peak of ecstasy, and the agony in my back and thighs drove me over the edge, and I cried out once more as my orgasm broke over me and my body shuddered.

Behind me, the king's throaty groan and animalistic grunt told me he was nearing his own climax, and I leaned against his grip, opening myself wider to his furious strokes. I moaned and panted with my release as he found his own climax, and I felt his cock throb as he emptied his seed deep inside me in hot spurts.

Gasping for breath, the king released his hold on my bound hands and eased me gently onto the bed. Still buried inside me, he leaned forward to untie my bonds, and as my arms fell down onto the bed, he thrust his hips forward, fucking into me again, lubed by his cum and my own slick heat. I tightened my body, milking his cock for every drop of cum before he withdrew from my soaking haven with a regretful moan.

I stayed in that position, my ass in the air, as the king stroked his hand over my burning flesh. The trickle of his seed down my thigh made me shiver, and I moaned as he swept the wayward liquid back into my pussy and pushed his fingers inside me.

"I will have a child," he said. "And if you perform this well every time we meet..."

"I will, Majesty," I moaned. His thumb swept over my aching clit, and I cried out into the coverlet as he pulled his hand away and allowed me to fall on my side on the bed.

"Liana," he murmured as he re-tied his breeches and washed his hands in the basin of water that had been left for me. "I will remember your name."

"Thank you, Majesty," I breathed.

He brought me the goblet of wine that he had been drinking from, and I sat up and brought it to my lips.

"You have earned a night of rest," he said. "But I shall return in the morning."

I nodded. I didn't know how often the king visited his concubines, but if he was as eager as Artin implied, perhaps this would be a daily occurrence.

I had to trust that my body would comply with my own wishes and that there would be a child before the new moon rose over the city. I had thirty days to prove my worth to him. Thirty days to make him never wish to be parted from me.

"Will you not stay, Majesty?" I asked.

He looked at me strangely and then chuckled. "Ambition looks well on you," he said, but he picked up the silver key from the table and unlocked the chamber door. As he departed, he looked back over his shoulder at me briefly before it closed.

I drained the cup of wine and hugged my knees to my chest. My whole body ached, but it thrummed with the intensity of my release and the knowledge that I had been chosen.

Me.

That I had made one of the Kings of the Jeweled Throne lose his composure. It had only been for a moment, but I had undone him just as easily as he had pulled me to pieces and then stitched me back together again.

My pussy throbbed, aching to be filled again.

If this was the side-effect of the goblin's tea, I wanted more. Would Artin get it for me if I asked? Or would I have to write to the goblin to beg for his herbs once more?

I scrambled off the bed and walked on unsteady legs toward the table that held the jug of wine and filled the cup again.

This time when I stood in front of the fire, the heat stung the places on my ass where the king had spanked me, and I relished the burn of it. He had marked me in more ways than one, and I yearned for his next visit with an eagerness that I hadn't anticipated.

The child might have been my goal, but I would enjoy making it, too.

5

———————

The room was still dark in the early hours of the morning, but it was the pressure of the bed moving beneath me that jostled me from sleep. Through the fog of my exhaustion and the stiffness in my limbs, I barely registered the warmth of bare skin against mine and the pressure of a hand as it smoothed over my side and down my flank.

The touch was familiar and sensual, and I arched back into it, moaning as long fingers caressed my pussy from behind and slid inside, first one, then two, moving in a gentle rhythm that I pressed into with a sleepy, languid eagerness.

Lips pressed against my shoulder and teeth bit down as I moaned and moved my leg to open my pussy to the pleasurable assault that was taking place.

"That's right," he murmured in a voice that sent shivers up my spine.

The thick head of the king's cock pressed against my pussy, and I arched back to encourage him. He pressed me down into the softness of the mattress and drove his cock deep into me with a choked groan.

"I shouldn't be here," he grunted. "But I could think of nothing but filling your womb with my seed—"

The furious pace of his strokes made me breathless, and the weight of his hand on my back trapped me against the mattress as he took me, hard and unrelenting. I didn't want softness. I wanted to be ravaged and used, and this king was a conqueror.

"Yes," I groaned as his hips slammed against my ass again and again. "Fill me, Majesty... put a child in my belly."

His cock twitched inside me and he let out a shuddering groan as he came, his hand tight on my ass. I pushed back against him, taking him deeper as the hot spurts of his cum filled my pussy.

He leaned forward and pressed his lips against my shoulder before he withdrew and left me panting on the bed.

"Artin doesn't know I'm here," he said as he pulled his tunic over his head and smoothed his dark hair back from his forehead. "I didn't have the patience for ceremony and propriety, but I wanted to fuck you before I went hunting."

"You do me great honor, Majesty," I said haltingly, and then smiled at him. "I hope you'll come again."

His smile was quick, and his eyes lingered on my breasts as I sat up on the bed. "I will," he said. "But not here. You'll be moved today. To a private residence."

"Private—"

"Until your pregnancy is confirmed, I shall breed you every day..."

"As your Majesty wishes."

He nodded and strode across the room and opened the secret door hidden behind one of the tapestries and disappeared from sight. The door closed with the softest creak of the hidden hinges, and I fell back on the bed and stared up at the embroidered canopy.

Was this how it always was with royal surrogates?

Or was it supposed to be a hardship—a chore... All I could think about was how my body responded to him, and how exquisite the king's cock felt inside me.

My heart had barely slowed its furious pace when the chamber door opened and Artin swept into the room, followed by several servants who set immediately to clearing it. Another servant grabbed hold of my wrist and dragged me from the bed. I stood in front of Artin, naked and shivering, as the bed was stripped.

She looked at me critically and then snapped her fingers sharply. A servant brought a robe and draped it over my shoulders, and I struggled into it without the woman's help.

"Did the king fuck you last night?" she asked.

My cheeks blazed with heat. "He did."

"To completion?"

"Yes."

She looked me up and down. "Did he stay the night?"

I shook my head, and Artin's lips twisted in a stiff smile. "I see."

"But he returned this morning—he was just here," I stammered.

Artin stepped close and thrust her hand between my thighs. I gasped and tried to flinch away, but she grabbed hold of my arm and held me firm. When she drew her hand away, I could see the remnants of the king's seed on her fingers. She rubbed them together and then wiped the slickness onto my robe.

"Good."

She released her hold on me, and I struggled to keep my balance.

"His Majesty has commanded that you be moved to the royal residence," she said briskly. "You are fortunate to be called for so soon. But I am not pleased by this change."

She clapped her hands, and the servants left the room with quick steps. When we were alone, Artin paced the carpet and then stopped and glared at me.

"You understand what this means?"

I shook my head.

"It means that the king is certain that he has already sired a child—you have precious little time to prove him right."

"I—" I hadn't realized that there was a limit to my time with him.

"If you are not pregnant, you will be cast out without a second thought, and I will not protect you."

"I need more of Tannyl's herbs," I blurted out. "Surely—"

Artin shook her head. "What you have taken should be sufficient. But you must make the king crave your body. You must make him insatiable for you. Can you do that?"

"I— I think so?"

Her hand flashed out and connected with my cheek. "You cannot think," she snarled. "You must."

I pressed my palm to my cheek and glared back at her. "Or what?"

"Or you will lose everything you have schemed your way to possessing," she hissed. "Do not think I do not know your designs. Some women come to me with the hope of being a surrogate to serve the kingdom, or for some misplaced love for their sovereign, or for the prestige it brings to a family to be so aligned with the royal house. But you... You do not want any of those things or have any of those high-born values."

My chin lifted in defiance.

"What does it matter?" I challenged her. "If the king puts a child in my belly, he gets what he wants, and I will get what I want."

Artin shook her head. "Your position is only possible because of me. And you would do well not to forget it. I can pull it all away in an instant."

My mouth was dry.

As bold as I thought I was, she was right. It would take no effort for her to destroy everything I had and leave me in the gutter with nothing.

"You will do as you are instructed," she said. It wasn't a question, it was a command. "Say that you understand me, Liana."

"I— I understand."

"Good," she snapped. "Wash yourself and get dressed. We have precious little time to follow the king's command."

❦

The rooms at the Monarch had taken my breath away and had prepared me in a small way for the luxury that I would enjoy as a surrogate. Fine food, rich wine, and anything I could want... but I wanted nothing. I had never had hobbies or pursuits beyond my work, and the realization that I would have nothing to occupy my time while I waited for the king to arrive filled me with a nervousness that I hadn't expected.

Artin pressed two wooden chests upon me before she left me in the care of the king's servants.

"Hide these," she hissed. "These are what you will need to inflame the king's lust for you, and to open your womb and make your ripeness even more potent. The seed of a king is powerful, but when paired with these... there will be a child."

I could only nod and accept the chests with a promise to hide them away.

"Follow the instructions that Tannyl has written for you, and we will see victory before the end of the month. Swear that you will do this."

I nodded. "Of course. This is all— this is all thanks to you."

Artin's smile never failed to chill me to the bone, and her pale eyes were hard as she looked at me. "Do as you are commanded, Liana. And pray to the celestial goddesses that you are not a waste..."

A waste.

I was worth nothing to them if I could not conceive.

I knew what the child would mean for me and for my future... But what was this child worth to them?

I was afraid to ask.

When she departed with her servants, I sat on the edge of the sumptuous bed and tried to make sense of the chaos in my mind. I wanted this—badly. Bad enough to risk my life and my future to attain it. The life I wanted was within my grasp.

A servant carrying a silver tray approached and handed me a goblet of wine that smelled sweeter than anything I'd ever tasted.

"Do you need anything, my Lady?"

"I— I am not a lady," I said.

"You are now," the girl replied.

Until the king tired of me, or if I was worthless...

"Washing water, I think," I said. I inhaled the scent of the wine and sighed happily as it enveloped me. Wildflowers and windswept berries… all the flavors of the wildwood and the history of our people.

"Of course," the servant said. "Have you looked at your gowns? His Majesty sent five trunks here this morning."

"Five?"

She nodded. "You must choose a favorite. I think you would favor the dark green… The embroidery would match your eyes very well. There are jewels as well."

"I—"

I stopped short of saying that I didn't deserve this finery. But this was what I wanted. I would have to get used to it. All of it.

It all felt so strange.

"I shall return with washing water shortly," the girl said.

"Is his Majesty—"

She paused. "The king is hunting with his brothers," she said. "They are not expected back at the palace for several hours."

"I see."

"The king will come and go as he pleases," the servant said. "You must not trouble yourself."

I nodded. As Artin had reminded me, I was a royal possession now, and he would use me as he saw fit.

Servants came and went, and I tried to ignore them as I pawed through the gowns that had been sent for me. Yards of gossamer watersilk, rich velvets, embroidered panels, and feathers… I could never choose my favorite. Or which order to wear them in.

Even the undergarments were made of fine, almost transparent material that I felt guilty pulling over my body.

The jewelry was just as overwhelming. For my hair, there were long strings of black pearls that had been taken from the shore of the orc territory on the opposite side of the inland sea—pearls bought with blood and sacrifice; I could almost see it in their oily depths.

Thick cuffs of intricately engraved silverblue set with moonstones fit over my wrists as though they had been made especially for me. The necklaces were beautiful, the purple-veined gold that was reserved for royalty set with large gems mined from the heart of the mountain below the citadel that housed the Jeweled Throne and the three kings who ruled over these lands.

But I couldn't wear them.

None of it felt right. It was all too heavy, and I didn't look like myself when I saw my reflection in the mirror.

The only piece of jewelry I couldn't remove was the sapphire chain that had been fastened around my hips. I could see its glint through the gossamer fabric of the shift I wore.

I'd tried to take it off, but the chain was fastened there by magic, and the only way it would come off was when my pregnancy had been confirmed. A powerful spell that could only be released by the change in my body...

An insurance policy.

The servant I'd sent away for washing water returned and set a large pottery jug down on a marble-topped table that held a large glass bowl. She pulled soft linen from a cupboard and set it beside the bowl.

She clapped her hands sharply. "Everyone out."

Her command echoed through the room, and the other servants gathered up their work and filed out of the room without so much as a backward glance.

I smiled gratefully as she refilled my wine goblet and left me alone to bathe.

I took a sip of wine and walked across the room to the bowl of steaming water. I savored the taste as it settled on my tongue and then set the goblet down upon the marble.

"Are you enjoying your new chambers?"

Venali Leonan's deep voice sent shivers down my spine and I spun around to find him. He stood in an arched doorway, leaning casually against the dark wooden frame like a rogue at a tavern. His dark eyes glittered in the soft light, and a nervous flutter twisted in my stomach. Resisting the urge to pull a robe around my shoulders, I stood up a little straighter and lifted my chin.

The gossamer fabric of the shift clung to my body, and his lips curved appreciatively.

"They are wonderful, thank you," I said. I didn't want to ask if every one of the potential breeders was given such beautiful accommodation.

"Finer than what you are used to?"

I could not stop the derisive snort that burst out, and the king's smile widened.

Embarrassed by my outburst, my stomach tightened. "That is... No, Majesty. I am not... I am still unsure..."

"Never feel as though you do not belong here," he breathed. "You were chosen above the others. Therefore, you belong."

He strode toward me, and I forced myself to stay still. This was the longest conversation we had shared, but I didn't know what I could ask, or what my position might be beyond the child that he wanted.

"May I pour you some wine, Majesty?" I stammered.

He inclined his head, and I rushed to the table to fill a

goblet for him. He took it from my shaking hands and watched me over the rim of the silverblue cup as he drank.

"Your scar," I blurted out. "How— How did it happen?"

His expression hardened for a moment, and then he set the goblet aside and stepped closer.

"In battle," he said in a voice that was darker than the wine in the goblet he had just set down. "An orc blade that came far too close for comfort."

"Oh," I murmured.

"You know nothing of war, do you?. No brothers or uncles sent away to fight for your king's armies—"

I shook my head and then lifted a hand to his face. He flinched as my fingertip traced the line of the scar, where it had split his bottom lip, and then traveled up his cheek.

"You must be fearsome in battle," I murmured.

He was only inches away from me, and I choked on a gasp of surprise as he caught my wrist in his hand and wrenched it away from his face.

"I am fearsome in many ways," he snarled.

I believed it.

"The servant said you were hunting," I said quickly, eager to change the subject. "I did not expect to see you—"

His eyes burned into mine, and I felt my throat grow dry as I read the raw passion in them.

"I had every intention of going hunting, but I could not concentrate on our preparations, nor on the plans for the hunt... all I could think of was you."

I swallowed hard, wondering if somehow he knew I had been thinking of him as well, if he could see on my face the lustful thoughts that I had, if he knew the heat that was between my thighs and how I yearned for his touch.

His eyes held me captive for a long moment before he

released his grip on my wrist. His arms wound around me and he crushed me to his chest and covered my lips with his in a kiss full of hunger and shameless passion.

I moaned and opened my mouth under his, gasping as his tongue thrust inside, probing and hungry. My body melted against his, and I could feel the hardness of his cock pressed against my stomach.

I wanted him so badly; wanted him to fill me with every inch of his hot length.

When he finally broke the kiss, my breaths were raw and his touch was like fire as he dragged his fingers along my collarbone and down the edge of the shift's neckline.

Beneath the transparent material, my breasts heaved, begging for his touch.

"When my brothers told me that I had to choose a surrogate, I didn't want to have the responsibility of it. Why was I forced to be the first? I thought it would be a chore—an assignment that I did not want or wish for. But now that you are mine, I find that I want you all the time."

With a quick motion, he tore the delicate fabric of my shift and dragged it down over my breasts. He bent his head to press his lips to the tender flesh, and my moan was ragged as he sucked at the pale skin that was exposed.

I could feel the heat between my thighs growing as he rubbed at my hardening nipples. My breath caught in my throat as the king ripped more of the shift away, and I shivered as it slithered down my body.

With a ragged sigh, the king's mouth latched onto one of the pink peaks, and I gasped and wound my fingers through his hair, pulling him closer, urging him to suckle harder. He caught my nipple between his teeth, and my gasp turned into a small cry as the pain and pleasure swirled in my stomach.

One of his hands gripped my other breast, pinching and tugging at the other nipple, and I could barely register all the sensations as they coursed through my body.

His free hand pushed the shreds of the shift down to the floor, exposing my heated flesh to the cool air. He dragged his mouth to my other breast and as his fingers found the slick wetness between my thighs.

He groaned deep in his throat and bit down gently on my already sore nipple. I gave a small cry, and it seemed to inflame him further, encouraging the force of his tongue and teeth on my swollen teat.

His fingers pushed inside me, gentler than they had the night before, as he caressed the hot center of my desire.

But I didn't want gentleness, not after the way his hard touch had made me feel, but this was what I craved.

My knees buckled, and the king released my breast to wrap his arm around me and pull me closer to his chest, supporting my weight as I sagged. His other hand remained busy between my thighs, stroking and teasing and dipping in and out of my soaking pussy, circling and plucking at my clit.

When I thought I could take no more, when my desire was at its peak and I could feel the edge of my release approaching, he stopped the motion of his fingers, and my cries of passion became a whimper of disappointment.

Without warning, he lifted his hand from between my thighs and pinched my hardened nipple between his thumb and forefinger. His fingers were slick with my juices, and my breast shone with wetness.

He rolled my nipple between his fingers, increasing the force of his grip by tiny fractions. His eyes were on my face, watching my reaction as I tried to process the sensations that tumbled through my body. The pain was almost too much to bear, but it was the pleasure and lust that followed close behind the pain that made me bite my lip, almost daring him to do more.

Seeing my confusion, pain and pleasure written plainly on my face, the king smiled and pinched harder before releasing and pinching again. I gasped at the change in pressure and cried out again when he flicked ever so gently at the tip of my tortured nipple.

I bit my lip, my eyes fixed on his fingers as they plucked and teased at my painfully hard nipples. If he continued much longer, I would reach my peak without feeling him inside me, and I wanted him inside me. I was hungry for him. I knew that my inner thighs were drenched and quivering. I was desperate for his hot length.

He rubbed his thumb in lazy circles over my nipple, making me gasp once more.

He gripped my breast gently, the hot nub of my tortured nipple pressing against the palm of his hand, and kissed me deeply before lifting me toward the bed.

"I want you like this for me always. Ready for me. Ripe. Wet and willing. Waiting for my command. Do you think about me when we are apart? Do you think about this," with his long fingers he spread the delicate folds of my pussy and rubbed his thumb over the pink flesh that quivered under his touch, "when you are alone... when your maid is helping you dress, perhaps?"

I shuddered with desire. It was as though he had known my very thoughts.

"Yes, Majesty... I do... I..." My words were cut off by a moan of desire as he spread me wide and gently slid his fingers into my pussy.

I moved my hips, meeting his thrusts eagerly, and

watched the look of desire on his face through half-closed eyes. His fingers stretched me, and I could not keep the groans of pleasure from escaping my lips.

All at once, he ceased the motion of his hand, and his fingers were replaced with the thick head of his cock. It pressed eagerly at my entrance, and I couldn't help myself from reaching for him, begging him with my eyes and my moans of pleasure to fill me up with every inch of his cock.

The king did not wait, and plunged the full length of his member inside me.

I cried out with the shock of it. He was large, and I could feel the stretch of my body as it rushed to accommodate him, and the pain from his rough treatment made me shudder with delight as the king's thighs slammed against me.

He took me hard and merciless and I was borne away on a tide of lust as I greedily accepted his powerful thrusts and urged him on with my cries, begging him for more, panting and gasping out my words.

The king hooked one of my knees with his hand and dragged it up higher close to his ribs as he changed his angle, driving deeper inside of me, and I cried out as his cock plunged into the deepest depths of my body. He moved faster, and his thumb flicked over my swollen clit, pinching and plucking at it until I was shuddering with the sensation.

The sensual torment was almost unbearable, and I was so close to my release, but I could not find the breath to beg for it yet.

The king pounded his cock into me as his thumb picked up speed, and my whimpers of pleasure and pain increased as he moved his thumb in circles to tease my feminine folds. His animalistic grunts of pleasure and conquest drove me closer to the edge, and I finally found the breath to gasp out my request.

His cock plunged deep. Mercilessly. And I careened toward the climax that was building deep inside me, and I feared it would carry me away. A groan shuddered between my lips as my body shivered with anticipation.

"Take your pleasure, Liana," he growled, "and I will fill you with my child while your pussy milks my cock for every drop."

With a cry of relief, I reached down between my thighs to feel his hardness as it stretched and plunged into my secret depths and found the tortured center of my desire.

As my fingers worked furiously at my clit, the tidal wave of my release crested and washed over me, and I tried to muffle the scream of pleasure with my hand as my body shook and pulsated with relief and release.

With a grunt of satisfaction as he felt my body clamping hard around his length, the king allowed his own release to overtake him, and I felt the pulse of his cock as he spilled his seed deep inside me.

He gripped my thighs hard, driving deeply inside me, claiming me as his own.

When his spasms had quieted, he leaned forward over my body and placed a tender, lingering kiss on my swollen lips before he withdrew and left me shuddering on the coverlet.

He washed himself quickly with the now tepid water that was still on the washstand and covered himself once more before dipping a linen cloth in the water and bringing it to the bed.

Tenderly he dragged the wet fabric over my bruised and

swollen flesh to clean away the sweat of lust and pleasure we had just shared.

I quivered and moaned as he washed my most intimate parts, and shuddered with pleasure as he traced his finger gently along my swollen folds.

"We cannot waste a single drop," he murmured as he pushed his fingers inside me to trap his cum there. "When your belly is round with my child, I can think back fondly on how it was conceived, with sweat and willing desire instead of duty."

Would that mean more to him? Did I mean more to him? I was afraid to ask.

He stared down at my body and traced his hand over my breasts and belly before he tugged on the jeweled chain around my hips. "I can scarcely believe that I can have you anytime I want you."

"Anytime, Majesty," I breathed.

6

———

I would be lying if I said I wasn't enjoying my trysts with the king. He was handsome and commanding, and he set my body alight with things I had never thought possible. I was eager for his visits and didn't want to think about what would happen when they stopped.

They would stop, one way or another.

The jeweled chain would fall from my waist to confirm my pregnancy, or I would be turned out into the street—worthless again.

I had done as Artin demanded, and the potions and powders she'd given me were gradually diminished as the days slipped by.

My official examination would be carried out at the end of the thirty days, but I'd hoped to be pregnant before then to secure not only the king's favor, but my own safety.

The king's visits were more frequent than I'd expected, and I wondered if the pregnancy he sought was more important than I was. No one had ever answered my question about what happened to surrogates after their pregnancy was confirmed and the child quickened.

My suspicions were difficult to push aside, but even when the king spent more time in my presence and even stayed the full night in my bed, I couldn't bring myself to ask him.

As winter approached and the threat of heavy snows hovered on the horizon, I started to count the days that remained. Every morning I tugged at the sapphire chain, hoping that it would fall away from my hips and clatter to the stone floor, but it held firm.

It was frustrating... I should have been pregnant already. The herbs, tea, potions, and powders should have seen to it.

Unless what Artin had given me was meant to keep me from becoming pregnant at all. That one thought set everything alight in my mind. Artin would suffer nothing if I failed to give the king a child. His Majesty would choose another young woman from a wealthy family and she would be richly rewarded for her continued support of the Jeweled Throne.

But I, the upstart servant girl from no bloodline of any importance, would be cast back to where I belonged. Artin would have her dominance once more, and I would be punished for daring to rise above the position that had been chosen for me by whatever celestial gods watched over us.

Suspicion dominated my thoughts, and I decided to ignore the instructions Artin had given me.

Three days passed and the strangeness I'd felt began to fade away, only to be replaced with something else.

One morning, as I stood in the marble basin that had been brought for my baths, the jeweled chain around my hips broke free and fell into the water.

As I bent to retrieve it from the water, one servant ran from the room. I stared at the chain, marveling at the richness of the rectangular jewels, while I tried to process what it meant for the clasp to release.

I was pregnant.

❦

"You should be moved to another suite in this building, but his Majesty has commanded that you be taken somewhere more... private."

"Private?"

Artin's expression was hard and unreadable as she paced the stone floor. I sat on the bed and stared down at my hands. The rich velvet dress I wore hugged every curve of my body as though it had been sewn directly onto my frame. The jeweled chain that had confined me had been re-worked into a necklace and was now hung with a large moonstone that dropped between my breasts. A symbol of the change in my status.

I could not help but feel a small stab of victory, as Artin seemed to struggle with her emotions. I had bested her.

"To the citadel," she said. "It is most unusual. When a surrogate is confirmed, she is moved to a quiet location so the pregnancy can be monitored properly to ensure that nothing goes awry. The king will then be able to return to his duties without the added burden of attending to the young woman that he chose. But if you are in the citadel—"

"Burden—"

· · ·

*V*enali had never treated me like a burden, or our coupling like a chore, and I refused to believe that he considered me a duty.

"Your position will change, of course, but Tannyl will be assigned as your doctor."

I looked up in surprise. "He will?"

Artin's lips pressed into a thin line.

"And what will happen to me after?"

"After? After what?"

"After the child is born."

Artin's bitter laughter filled the room. "The child will be well cared for. It will be a ruler of this great kingdom. That is the price."

"And what about me?"

"You?"

My fingers twisted in my lap. "Me. What happens to me? There is a harem for the royal surrogates, isn't there? Somewhere for them to live out their days in luxury and comfort?"

"Is that what you believe?"

My throat was tight.

"Is it not true?"

Artin came closer, and I could smell the richness of her perfume. "There is no such place. Could you imagine the cost of such a thing? The kingdom would never allow it. No surrogate survives the birth of a royal child."

Her voice was a hiss, and every word chilled me to the bone.

"You're lying," I whispered.

"Am I?" she said. "Do you love the king?"

"I—"

Venali fucked me like he loved me... and my heart had betrayed me on far too many occasions to deny that I loved him. The way I felt around him was inescapable. It could be nothing else but love.

"Consider it carefully," Artin said. "Perhaps there is a way that your life might be spared."

I swallowed hard. "What do you mean?"

"I will say no more of it now," she replied. "But you would be well advised to forget your ridiculous dreams. Your life matters only as long as you carry that child in your belly. Afterward—"

Her voice trailed away and left an ominous silence in its wake. She was threatening me, but at the same time warning me. I didn't know what it meant, only that everything had changed. The only security I had ever known had been ripped out from under me, and I was adrift.

Artin straightened and brushed her hands over her watersilk bodice. "The servants will come to take you to your new chambers," she said. "Keep your worries to yourself. Tannyl and I will work on your behalf."

"And I am to trust that you will?"

Artin's smile was as cold and empty as her eyes. "Of course," she said. "You are our responsibility. Where would you be if it were not for us?"

As she swept from the room, I couldn't decide if her words were a threat or a promise, or a mixture of both. Whatever the truth was, I was in danger.

7

In a secluded wing of the citadel just below the royal quarters, the first months of my pregnancy passed in relative solitude. My only visitors, aside from the constant stream of servants who granted my every request without question, were Tannyl and the king. Artin did not visit or check on my progress herself, and I was grateful for it. I didn't think I could look at her face or listen to her smugly cold voice without reacting ever again.

I was surprised that the frequency of Venali's visits did not change, but I didn't know what I should have expected. Perhaps Artin's words had done their work, and I was surprised when he did not forsake my bed or his interest in my changing body.

With the birth only weeks away, my nervousness returned.

During his visits to check the progress of the pregnancy, Tannyl had repeated Artin's warning about what happened to the surrogates after the birth—they were never heard of again, or seen in the kingdom. Surely, it wasn't hard to believe that they were dispatched or even banished in return for their sacrifice.

In the night, as the moon rose high above the citadel, I turned to darker thoughts. Venali's steady breathing and the sound of spring rain against the chamber window should have comforted me, but all I could think of was what would happen to me after the child was born.

Could he really cast me out or allow my life to end... after all we had shared—

"What is it?"

His voice was slow and steady, and undulled by sleep. He had been awake listening to me sigh and squirm.

"The child," I murmured. "Your son is restless tonight."

His warm hand slipped over my hip and rubbed over the roundness of my belly.

"You're lying," he murmured. "The babe is dreaming of his first day in the spring air, as you should be."

Tears pricked my lashes, and I blinked them away. Tannyl and Artin would have me believe that I would never see my son's first breaths or hear his first cry.

"I am trying," I said.

"You have been distracted," he said. "Is there nothing I can do?"

Without meaning to, I grabbed his arm, and then had to physically hold myself back from tugging him over me. It was a ridiculous notion when I couldn't even lie fully on my own stomach anymore. He rose up on his elbow to kiss me, and I could only hope that I could distract him from my worries with the promise of my body.

His hand moved to cup my neck, thumb rubbing circles on my tender flesh. The feel of his fingers was different.

Larger and thicker, less intense than the scorching heat of his mouth.

I sighed into his kiss with pleasure and gripped his shoulder tight. His knee was between my legs, a comforting weight without being demanding. When his mouth left mine to move down the curve of my neck, I had no breath to protest and squeezed my thighs together as he licked his way down to my collarbone.

"Venali," I hissed as I gripped the back of his neck.

"Yes?" he asked, still rubbing my neck with his fingers. I had expected him to move of his own accord down my body. Yet, he hadn't, and that left my full breasts aching, wanting attention.

The king smiled as he tugged at the ribbon that held my shift closed, and as the fine material fell away, he drew a breath in between his teeth and then his mouth closed over the exposed peak of my nipple.

He groaned as he suckled at my breast, and I let out a soft moan as my back arched in response.

My breasts were so sensitive, and I felt an immediate pang to know that my swollen nipples were leaking milk. But the king seemed not to care, and the press of his hard cock against me did not signal any reluctance on his part.

Before, my breasts had just felt heavy and sore, but his swirling tongue was nearly too intense.

I was trembling all over already, and he had barely started; I tried to pull him closer. "Oh, stop, stop, don't stop!"

To his credit, he did not heed my pleas, instead drawing his hand over my other breast to massage it lightly with his palm, the slickness of my milk only lubricated his attentions and I moaned and gasped, pushing and twisting readily into his hand, as well as I could with my swollen belly.

His hand moved to caress the roundness of my stomach as he sucked gently on one nipple. The feel of his hand on my belly while his mouth teased and inflamed my breasts left me torn; reminding me all at once that I was large with child and yet... the overpowering want for him had her tight in its grip.

The ache I felt for him had only grown sharper as my pregnancy advanced, and I could not stop my yearning for him any more than I could stop the rain that drove against the chamber window.

The king flicked his tongue over the hard peak of my nipple, and then bit down lightly around the dusky pink bud, drawing a hard moan from my lips.

"Oh please," I whimpered, thighs opening. It was almost embarrassing how quickly I was reduced to squirming desperation under his touch.

His hand slid down the side of my stomach, agonizingly slow, to the taut skin below, and he brushed his fingers against my pussy gently before brazenly cupping my sex.

"Here?" he teased.

Of course, I should have known that he couldn't resist, but my only answer was another shaking moan. I knew I was slick and ready for him, and when he slid a finger inside me, I cried out softly and whimpered for more.

Each stroke of his long fingers, combined with the suction of his mouth on my breasts, had me desperately clutching at his shoulders.

"Yes," I answered the question he didn't ask. "Yes, more. I need you!"

His hand went still, causing me to whimper in frustration. "Are you sure?" he asked carefully. His hard cock pressed against my thigh was proof enough that he must want the same thing, and his consideration made my heart lurch in my chest. Perhaps he loved me.

"Yes," I gasped, "now."

He smirked as he always did at my demands, and he gripped a breast with one hand as he adjusted me to my side and facing away from him. I moaned at the loss of contact, uncertain why he was moving me away.

But when he pressed his hard cock against the back of my thighs, I stopped squirming.

"Oh!" I murmured, surprise and desire raging through me as he let out a grunt and tore the gossamer fabric of my shift away from my body and threw it to the floor. He lifted my knee and then pushed between my thighs, but not inside me yet. It seemed almost cruel for him to tease me when I was so desperate for him, and I groaned wordlessly in frustration.

"Let me savor it just for a moment." He chuckled against my shoulder and I bit down hard on my cheek to keep myself in check. Yet, he had mercy and pressed the firm head of his cock against my silken folds, finally, finally pressing in.

It seemed to take forever for him to sink himself fully inside me, and then he went still. I nearly sobbed aloud at the halt in his motion.

"I need just a moment." He kissed my back and shoulders, fingers caressing and plucking at my aching nipples, once again tugging warm liquid from them to lubricate his furiously sensual movements.

Moving his hand from my knee, he slid his hand below my belly to stroke his fingers against the swollen slickness of my clit. He teased and fondled me expertly, drawing gasps and moans from my lips with no effort. As the waves of pleasure built inside me, he moved his hips.

Open-mouthed, I panted for him, pushing back against

him as well as I could to meet his every thrust. His other hand, cradling me against his chest, was still rubbing at the swollen buds of my nipples as he moved inside me. His breathing was already deep and ragged, and the sound of it drove my arousal higher. A King of the Jeweled Throne, undone by my body... It was a raw and powerful realization.

"Let go," he groaned against my skin, "I need you to..." The deep sound of his desire for me went straight through me and combined with his skillful touch, he had me spiraling out of control.

My skin prickled all over, already heavy and hot. The burning sensation deep inside me swept throughout my body until I felt consumed by it.

At the apex of my ecstasy, I cried out and grabbed for his arm as my body tightened and trapped him inside me.

The king gasped as I clamped down on his cock and he thrust hard enough to make me cry out in pleasure once more before he groaned deep in his throat and filled me with hot seed.

Whimpering with release, I clutched his arm against my leaking breasts, dizzy and overcome with emotion and passion.

It felt like hours passed before a hazy exhaustion sank into my sated limbs and I held his arm securely, glad he was still inside me. He would pull away in a moment to clean away our sweat and the remnants of our passion, as he used to, but for now, I basked in the feel of his body against mine.

The king's touch roamed over the swell of my stomach and over my changed body; luxuriating in it. I had never felt more beautiful or desired than I did at that moment, which only brought the reason for my suspicions and fears careening back at a terrifying speed.

"What will happen after the child is born?" I whispered.

"What do you mean?" His words were soft, and I could feel the hammering of his heart against my back.

"What will happen to me?"

Lips pressed to my bare shoulder. "What do you think will happen?"

"I— I don't know."

"What did Artin tell you?"

Heat flared in my chest. "I don't want her answers. I want yours." My words sounded angry, and perhaps I was.

Why wouldn't anyone give me an answer?

Venali's breath was warm against my back and his fingers were gentle on my belly. "What do you want to happen?"

"I— I don't want to be sent away," I blurted out. "I want to raise our child and watch him grow. Please say you will not release me and forget me."

There was silence for a moment, and then Venali's arm tightened around me and pulled me back against his chest once more, trapping me there. His hips moved slightly, driving his cock deep inside me once more. He was still hard, and I bit down on my lip to keep from moaning.

"Did you think I would be able to cast you aside?" he whispered.

"I—"

"I will fuck you until the last day of my life," he growled. "Our children will fill the citadel and put my brothers to shame with their beauty."

His cock twitched inside me as the king's hand fell upon

my hip and held me tight. He thrust up into me, building a gentle rhythm.

"I want no one else to bear my children. Only you."

I moaned and pushed back against him, encouraging him to drive his cock into me harder and faster until I was panting and moaning with the exquisite pleasure of it.

"You belong to me, Liana," he growled, and he bit down on my shoulder. The sudden flash of pain made me cry out, and my nails dug into his forearm as my climax crested and broke over me.

Venali groaned as my body tightened around his cock, and I moaned with him as his hard length pulsed inside me, filling me with his seed again.

"Do you believe me?" he asked, his voice heavy with desire.

"I do," I replied.

And I did. I believed him.

❧

I felt like a fool for believing that I would be harmed or cast out of the kingdom once my duty was done... And that feeling only grew when the king took me to the royal harem. Venali's mother, another royal surrogate, lived in luxury and refinement, a position promised to every woman who bore a fae king.

"You will be well cared for," he assured me as we walked together in the citadel's quiet corridors. The gardens outside were in full bloom, and the trees were heavy with blossoms and nesting birds. Spring had always brought nothing but dread to my life—wet feet, moldy blankets, and an impossible amount of work. But now that I was at the citadel? Spring had become my favorite time of year.

"How could you have believed otherwise?" he asked.

"I— I do not know. No one told me what it would be like..."

"And you guessed that the worst would happen?"

I shrugged. "I have known nothing else."

The king's arm snaked around my thickened waist, and he hugged me to his side. "You shall never know anything but kindness here," he said. "I promise it."

The glow of his promise stayed with me, even in the darkest parts of the night, and I refused to think about the lies that Tannyl and Artin had told me.

But the child's birth was imminent, and my appointments and examinations had increased, which meant I was forced to be in the goblin's company far more often than I liked. His examinations were always rough and painful, and I couldn't shake the feeling that something terrible was about to happen every time he arrived at the citadel.

"Your child is growing quickly now," the goblin said. "The birth pains will be upon you in a few days' time."

"So soon?"

My fear of what lay ahead of me had been replaced by my fear of the pain and blood that would bring this child into the world. What if I didn't survive? Women died in childbed all the time. My own mother had not survived my birth... I had barely survived it.

"We have not spoken of our agreement in some time," Tannyl said.

"Agreement—"

The goblin's eyes glittered in the candlelight. "You could not be here without my help."

"I don't owe you anything," I whispered.

"Don't you?"

My mouth was dry and my throat was tight. I did owe him... without his help, I would never have been brought into the Monarch. I would never have been presented to Venali. He never would have chosen me.

"What do you want?" I pulled a jeweled comb from my hair and held it out to him. "Gold? Jewels? I can get you whatever you want."

The goblin's ink-stained fingers tapped on the edge of the table that held his herbs and potions. "Can you? What I want has no sparkle, girl."

"Then what?"

"Your son will be a king, but if something were to happen to his Majesty before the child comes of age, a regent will be required."

"A regent—"

I knew nothing of politics or the scheming that occurred behind the scenes of power.

"You must do something for me," he said. He pulled an iron key from his pocket and unlocked an iron-bound wooden chest. The click of bottles filled the air as he dragged his fingers through the contents of the box and then selected one. He drew out a dark blue glass vial sealed with black wax.

"What is that?"

"A guarantee," he said. "You will give this to the king. In his wine. Or in his food. Put it on your pussy for all I care... just see that he takes it all."

"And the child?"

"You don't need to worry about that. As soon as the child is born, you won't have to think about it ever again.

You'll be free, and Artin will see that you're well taken care of."

Free.

But would I be? What if he was lying?

I stared at the vial and then pushed myself off the examination bed. "I will not. I will not do anything to harm the king. And I will not give up my child."

"You made a pact, girl," the goblin growled.

"I won't do it."

The vial disappeared into the chest and the lock clicked shut. "You'll regret this."

I wrapped my arms protectively around my belly. "You need to leave," I said stiffly. "And tell Artin I do not wish to see her again."

The goblin snorted and packed his chests away into the wagon that he brought with him to each examination.

"We shall see," he growled.

Without waiting for him to say another word, I turned on my heel and fled the room. I needed to find solace in Venali's arms. And I needed to tell him what had happened. They had wanted me to harm him. And it might have worked. If I had not been shown what would happen to me, or if I had been left to believe the terrible lies that I had been told, I might have been desperate enough to do something stupid...

I might have done it.

I might have killed him.

But everything was different now.

I loved him.

And my future was secure.

I needed to tell him everything.

8

———

The pains began early in the morning before the birds had begun to sing. My screams of pain brought Venali and his guards running through the stone corridors of the citadel, and he found me on the floor, hands clasped around my belly as the tremors of the birthing pains ripped through me.

"Tannyl is coming," he said as he lifted me in his arms and held me tight against his chest.

"Where— where are we going?" I choked out.

"You will give birth to the next royal son of the Leonan line in my bed," he said. "And then you will not leave it again."

"But, Majesty," one of his advisors said, clearly shocked, "she must be taken to the birthing chambers. It is tradition."

"It is no longer my tradition," Venali snarled.

The advisor nodded, and I felt a swell of love for the king who had taken me into his heart, as well as his bed.

"I need to tell you something," I whispered as he laid me down on the rich coverlet. Servants rushed into the room with hot water and towels, and a cool cloth was pressed to my forehead.

"What is it?"

"Tannyl," I whispered. "The goblin. Do not let him near me. He has... He has threatened to steal the child away and plans to end your own life. Please, please do not let him in."

Venali's dark eyes narrowed. "Why would he do what?"

"I defied him. I refused to do his bidding."

"His bidding? I don't understand."

Desperation clawed at me with sharper pangs than my impending delivery. "The only reason I was presented to you is because of the goblin... I would never have been considered as a surrogate without his help. I promised—"

The tears came in a flood.

Venali took hold of my chin and forced me to look at him. "It doesn't matter what you promised. He doesn't own you."

I shook my head. "Not anymore."

Venali's forehead creased in anger and I worried I had said too much. Pain rippled across my stomach, and I cried out in agony.

"Please," I choked out, "do not let him in. I do not need his potions. I only need you."

"The goblin is here, Majesty," a servant said. "He brings medicine and herbs to ease the surrogate's birth."

"Take the potions from him and have the guards take him to the dungeon," the king commanded without looking at the servant who had spoken. He took my hand in his and held it gently.

"Majesty, are you—"

"Do not make me repeat myself!" he shouted. The servants scrambled to do his bidding and the thud of the guards' boots on the stone floor filled me with fear for a split second before the chamber door slammed shut. Shouts from the corridor confirmed that the king's command had been followed.

"You are safe with me," he said, and leaned forward to kiss me. His lips were tender, and I leaned into his kiss with relief and wonder. He loved me... I knew it with every inch of my body, and when the kiss broke, his smile lifted my heart even higher..

"Now, my darling, Liana, let us welcome our son into the world."

THE END

CONTINUE YOUR JOURNEY TO KRATERRA WITH THE FAE SURROGATES SERIES!

KRATERRAN KINGDOMS

ORC WARLORD

Orc's Unwilling Bride

Orc's Captive Bride

Orc's Vengeful Bride

***

ORC REBEL

Betrayed by the Orc

Claimed by the Orc

Rescued by the Orc

***

ORC BROTHERHOOD

Protected by the Orc

***

FAE SURROGATES

Betrayed by the Fae King

Stolen by the Fae King

***

STANDALONE NOVELS

Wild Heart

Kraterran Kingdoms

www.ingramcontent.com/pod-product-compliance
Lightning Source LLC
Chambersburg PA
CBHW052209150726
48002CB00003B/1144